USHERED

Yet Abandoned

The Mask of a First Lady

VANESSA RODGERS TRACY

For information contact: www.vanessartracy.com

Front Book Cover :   Charles Beason
                        www.charlesbeason.net

Back Book Cover & Interior Layout Design:
Enger Lanier Taylor for In Due Season Publishing
www.indueseasonpublishing.com
indueseasonpublishing@gmail.com

ISBN: 978-0972745635

Photographer: Charles Beason
Makeup Artist: Sylvia Smith
Hair Stylist: Tonia Renee` Lampley

CONTENTS

Foreword

There are people who say they will do something. Then, there are people who actually do it. Vanessa Tracy is the latter. Not only is she a woman of action, but also she is a woman of compassion, perseverance, and most importantly love. This book, in both her commitment to bringing it to life and the storyline itself, is one example of the way she loves.

Ushered Yet Abandoned: The Mask of a First Lady will bring a revelation for some, healing for others and a mirror for those who might see themselves and their lives reflected on the pages.

As a reader of this book, be prepared to receive a front seat view into the often untold lives of the people in the pulpit, particularly the pastor's wives. Until this point, you may have seen them as models of perfection. This story will help you to see them as they truly are; human and perfectly imperfect. Vanessa's writing is transparent and honest, might make you shed a tear, and will surely elicit a laugh. It is everything you would expect from a woman whose faith in God is much stronger than those who may have attempted to break her.

I am so very proud of Vanessa for setting pen to paper, and I am looking forward to hearing about the lives revived and changed by her words.

Dwaynia Wilkerson
Prose + Pens

Foreword

The author of this book (Vanessa Rodgers Tracy) does an excellent job bringing fictitious characters to life and addressing issues that anyone who has ever been in a relationship, whether it was a marriage, a friendship or a work relationship, has faced at some point and time.

As a former First Lady, the author is able to boldly address issues that only someone who has held this much-coveted title can attest. Her strength, motivation, and resilience to overcome and surpass disappointments, hurt and rejection gives her the ability to write from a personal place.

This book is a great read for anyone who has struggled with forgiveness and/or truly wants to know whether or not it is really possible to forgive and move forward. The answer, as this author so elegantly expresses, is "YES!" There is life after every storm and hurdle.

I could never be more proud of you Mom. You continue to excel in all areas of your life, and you are the embodiment of what many strive to be, a virtuous woman.

Melody S. Holt
Motivational Speaker/Author

PART 1
First Lady Speaks

CHAPTER ONE
Before The Mask

Tucked into bed and sound asleep, Nana and Papa lay contently next to one another happy just to be alive and together. Never had I witnessed a love so strong, that it withstood the tests of time, temptation, and the taint of illness, as theirs. I stood propped against the doorframe and stared at them in wonder, eagerly anticipating the day this kind of love would be mine. I looked down at the chastity band on my finger, sighed deeply, and went to the living room to catch up on some much needed rest.

Once comfortable in my usual spot on the sofa, I looked intently at the band on my finger. I slowly wound it about as I reminisced on the day I gave this part of my life completely to God. No more would I be used or misused. No more would I make mistakes when it came to choosing a mate. No more would I give my heart to the wrong man because I would first learn to give my heart to the giver of love; the One who *is* love.

The chastity band on my wedding finger was a constant reminder of the vow I had made to God two years prior. I was His, and He was mine. I vowed to be His perfect bride, and He promised to be my husband. He promised to provide for me, to protect me, and to love me. I knew this because some time ago, in a dream, He had spoken to me and said, "The man who removes this band from your finger will be a mighty man because he will be chosen by Me."

Yes, God and I were one, and I loved it. My steps were truly ordered by Him, and it was His arms that held me close. It was His voice that whispered, "I love you" in the middle of the night and it was His hands that stroked my face in the morning to wake me up. The smile on my face was a direct result of Him and our spiritual adventures.

As Nana and Papa's overnight caretaker for several years, I had grown to love them like my own parents. I watched as their health declined, but their spirits soared, and their love grew deeper by the day. The lessons I learned from them far outweighed the time away from my own home and family.

Watching the love that Nana and Papa shared was a joy for me. They had been together for over 60 years, and the love had not died. Theirs was the kind of marriage taught in the Bible. It was the kind I longed to have one day. Papa never passed Nana's bed without telling her he loved her or teasing her by grabbing her toes and saying, "Oh I could just eat those little toes up!"

Nana would giggle and say, "Oh darling, I love you!"

They had shared the story of how they met many times. Every time I heard it, I stopped to listen as if it was the first time. Nana was 15 years old, and Papa was immediately taken by her beauty, but being the gentleman he was, he knew to tread cautiously.

See, Nana and Papa met during a time when men were respectful and did not dare expect too much of a woman too soon. A woman was a delicate flower and the thought of doing anything to dishonor her was unthinkable. Conversations were held with the utmost respect, and if they held hands, it was counted as an honor. I would often ask Nana why she took the time to stop and talk to Papa on that fateful day by the railroad tracks and she would smile and say, with an elevated voice, "Because he was handsome!"

Every night Papa and Nana shared stories of their life together, and once I tucked them both into bed for the night, we would have devotion and prayer. Nana could pray with such power. She wasn't loud or aggressive, but the words she used when she prayed could only come from a woman who knew the Lord. Despite battling several illnesses, Nana still had a relationship with God like none other. It wasn't long before Papa would start leading the prayer and, according to Nana, his praying became stronger.

We always started the devotion by singing "Jesus Loves the Little Children," Nana's favorite and then "Yes Jesus Loves Me," Papa's favorite. The Twenty-Third Psalm was always the scripture of choice, and although Papa was in the early stages of dementia, he had no problem reciting the chapter. Oftentimes, I would have him to recite it to keep his memory sharp.

After wading through the fond memories of the sweetly divine couple in the other room, I looked back at the chastity band on my finger. I sighed deeply and thanked God that for all these years I had been blessed to glean from Nana and Papa. I didn't have to wonder what love looked like because it was right there in front of me and I felt fully nurtured at that moment. I drifted off to sleep with a smile, my heart full of thanksgiving.

I awoke the next morning to the sound of Papa yelling, "coffee time!" Tired, but content, I tended to Nana and Papa, gave the daytime caretaker the usual updates, and headed back to my house to shower and change for my day job. There would be no time for my morning walk, and I was forced to have my devotion and morning worship in the car.

It was the start of a new workweek, a time to begin a fresh and new experience serving God in this area of my life. I had grown accustomed to being a servant. My life was full to the brim because I was always pouring out of myself. I was constantly making room for God to fill me and to give me the desires of my heart; which consequently, always went back to giving more of myself. Because mine was not dry, duty-bound service, I never grew weary in well doing. Though I sometimes got tired in body, my mind was always at peace, and the joy that filled my heart was evident to others, so it was easy for me to draw love into my life. I just wanted it to be the right kind of love. I wanted a forever love like what I witnessed with Nana and Papa.

I had come to be rather proud of the patience my chastity band with God had taught me. It was as if all the things in the world that once mattered when it came to love were not so important. What mattered most was that my future relationship and marriage would be pleasing to God. For this, I was willing to wait and to allow Him to renew my strength day by day.

I learned as much as I could from Nana and Papa by taking note of their fond memories of one another and making mental notes to be sure to create loving memories with my future husband. I dreamed about a time when I, Minister Viveca Reece, would change my last name and become one with the man whom the Lord would send to bring His name glory through our union.

As I arrived home, showered, changed, ate breakfast, and drove to work, I couldn't help but sing praises, recite scriptures out loud, and bask in the glow of God's promises to always love me and never to leave nor forsake me. The rising of the morning sun and feeling the warmth on my face was confirmation that God was there with me.

I thought deeply as I pulled up to work and shut off the car engine. What a clearer sense of myself I had gained over the past two years. I was no longer a stranger to the woman in the mirror. I was healed from the pain of my first marriage. Genuine in my faith, I was now free to be myself with everyone I encountered. For the first time in forty years, I could say I was one hundred percent happy with my life. I whispered my morning pre-work prayer as I got out of the car, "God, whatever your plans are for me today, let me not get in the way of them. For this day I pray, not my will but your will be done. Make this day what you would have it to be and help me to do those things pleasing in your sight. In Jesus' name. Amen."

CHAPTER TWO

Pretty Woman

At 40 years old, I was one of the associate ministers at Mt. Sharon Missionary Baptist Church in a small town called Clearville, Alabama. Under the leadership of my spiritual father, Reverend L. R. Sims, I was being groomed in protocol as a female minister in a Baptist society dominated by men. In spite of that, I had managed to win over the naysayers and gain the trust and respect of an older generation who had once abhorred the idea of a woman in the pulpit.

See, I had discovered that my position did not define me. I was Minister Viv in the pews, I was Minister

Viv on my job, I was Minister Viv in the grocery store, I was Minister Viv at home, and most of all I was Minister Viv when no one else was looking; when it was just God and me.

I did not take it for granted when I gained the respect of a brother or sister in Christ. It was too precious of a gift, and God was teaching me the true meaning of Matthew 7: 16-20, *"Wherefore by their fruits ye shall know them."* God was being an awesome husband to me, and I was making sure I was sowing good seeds.

There were many challenges and times that I had to truly remember who I was and to whom I belonged. As a legally single sister, I quickly learned it was not unusual for someone to believe they were in love with me without realizing that it is the *Jesus* in me that they were drawn to, not Minister Viv. After all, they did not know me. Jesus is the drawer. He has the power to make people feel what they have never felt and the ability to introduce them to true love.

It can be earth shaking for those who are feeling this type of pull for the first time. They can be misguided into believing they are experiencing something natural between a man and a woman. Add to that feeling the fact

God made us this way, and you have a perfect storm brewing if you do not remain spiritual.

Before we come into the realization of who Christ really is, because we as a people are maneuvered by emotions, it is no surprise that in our weakest moments we become attached to what lifts us up and gives us hope. I had often heard of the Stockholm Syndrome where a person had been taken captive by someone who totally meant them evil and did evil things to them, but they became attached to their captor. I could not fathom that in my mind at the time, but when I started seeing it in my spiritual calling, it became very perceptible.

I could preach a message, and someone would fall in love with me. I could spend a little time with someone, encouraging them, and they would fall in love with me. I would be a spiritual ear to someone, and they would fall in love with me.

I quickly learned that we as ministers of the gospel had to be very careful and to handle these precious souls that God has entrusted us with delicately and to make sure we did not cross the lines that God had established for us. I very promptly made it clear to them that they were only in love with the Jesus they saw in me and it was the Spirit of the Lord drawing them to Him and not to me. Some would eventually come into that realization, and I was able to assist them still. With others, I had to form a barrier limiting their access to me because I realized they were becoming more infatuated with the vessel instead of the Spirit within the vessel.

God soon showed me this was one of the reasons He had become very displeased with so many of His shepherds. They had become infatuated with the attention and affection of lost and wounded sheep and had taken advantage of the precious souls they were to lead to Him. Instead, many of them had devoured the sheep with the lust of their own flesh and had done so in His name. They became deceivers of their own selves and workers of iniquity instead of fishermen. I was determined not to be named amongst that number, and even though the revelation was frightening, I thanked God for it.

So there I was, living Deuteronomy 28:13. I was the head and not the tail, above and not beneath, the lender and not the borrower. It seemed as though everything I touched was turning to gold. All I had to do was desire it, and it manifested itself. I am not just talking about money, even though I had plenty. It could be something as simple as wanting flowers to plant in my flower garden, and someone would bring me some, out of the blue, from their garden. Many things came to me in the way of favor. God probably knew he couldn't give me too much money because I would have become an enabler instead of a helper.

Now, do not think all this goodness was coming to me because I had always done the right thing. Before I accepted Christ as my Lord and Savior, I made some horrible decisions. Some were out of ignorance, and some were out of survival. I always had morals and values, but I found myself in some situations that resulted in me compromising those morals and values at times. Certain situations tested who I was. Sometimes I passed the test and sometimes I failed. The funny thing is God definitely has a "get right" type of personality. If you failed the test, it was sure to come up again, and no real progress was made until you passed. Yes, God and I were one. He was teaching me, and I was loving Him.

I had always been a modest person who loved the simple things in life, so it did not take much to maintain my lifestyle. I figured the excess financial favor God blessed me with was to give to others. I got great joy in knowing I had made someone's day. I probably benefited the most from uplifting a hung down head, placing a smile on a sad face, or encouraging a wounded spirit. It was my pleasure giving hope where there was none and most of all helping someone to see Jesus.

My weekends were spent visiting the sick and shut-in and nursing homes. It did not take much to make the people I encountered in those places happy. A bag of fruit, a balloon, or simply cutting their toenails and fingernails made their day. I enjoyed doing for them what they were no longer able to do for themselves.

I had no problem sitting on floors that most people would be reluctant to walk barefoot on and I never wore fancy clothes because to me it made the visits too impersonal. As I pulled out my tools to wash their feet and cut their nails, some would apologize for their feet being in such poor condition, and I would respond by saying, "Your feet are not bad, they just need a little work."

I never wore gloves because I wanted the visits to be very personal. Besides, while I was doing their feet and making contact, I was praying for God to heal them. I prayed for God to add life to their years and most of all draw them closer to Him. I prayed that their latter days would be greater than their first.

My life was perfect, and I could not even imagine it getting any better. I was a virtuous woman, happily living out my singleness. I felt whole, stable, useful and full of purpose. Then *he* came back into my life and things quickly changed. What is a pretty woman to do when the God of everything, who knows the beginning and the end, allows an experience that could wrench all the beauty of holiness from her soul? What is a virtuous woman to do when the man who once ushered her into the presence of the Most High, now only ushered in a well of broken promises? How could I, a whole woman, fall for such a broken man?

CHAPTER THREE

The Last Call

H ello, Sister Viv. Pastor Thomas Brand here. How are you?"

"Doing fine, Pastor. How are you?"

"Well, to be perfectly honest Sister, not so good. I was wondering if I could unplug at your place for a few days. I need to get myself together. My soul is tired, Sister."

"I understand, Pastor. I will be teaching at Bible study tonight at seven. You can come after I get off at five and I can get you settled in before I have to leave if that's okay?"

"That's perfect. Except I don't have a ride there."

I paused for a moment. I wou
time to get to his town and back befc
church. I calculated the risk of being
mental state. I estimated that if I left wor.
five, I could be back just as the opening so   .. prayer
were finishing. I hated being late for church but figured it
was worth it this one time.

"Okay, I can be there by six o'clock. Is that okay?"

"Yes, Sister. I'll see you then. Thank you. You are
such a blessing."

"Always, Pastor. Just glad to be of service."

During the day, from 8:00 am to 5:00 pm, five
days a week, I was an administrative assistant for a local
forestry company. The owner of the company, Mr.
Miller, was a devout Christian which made for a very
pleasant atmosphere at work. Mr. Miller hired me while
I was still attending college and had worked around my
school schedule. When I graduated, he gave me a full-
time position and the two of us had become an awesome
duo. Mr. Miller and his wife, Cherry, had welcomed me
into their lives and we all spent a lot of time together
away from the office.

I hung up from my call with Pastor Brand to find

Miller looking at me with a confused, yet concerned look on his face. You see, Mr. Miller was not only my employer and business partner, but he was also like a father figure. We had learned each other over the years and could tell when something wasn't quite right with the other. I had spent many nights praying for him and Cherry as they faced challenges with their adoptive boys. Mr. Miller and his wife had made my move to Clearville a more pleasant one, and through them, I had met some wonderful people.

I assured Mr. Miller that everything was alright. I'd been dealing with Pastor Brand long enough to know that he was just a helpless soul in need of support. Besides, I had been taught growing up that you never messed with the man of God. I had the utmost respect for his position as a pastor and would never cross that line; that was just a no-no as far as I was concerned. Mr. Miller told me he was proud of me for always showing Christian love and walked back to his office.

I finished the day with a bit of anxiety. I didn't know why at first. I thought it was the idea of having to rush to pick up Pastor Brand and be back in time to teach Bible study. Later, as I drove the fifty miles to Pastor

Brand's apartment, I thought back on Mr. Miller's concern. I had known him for over eight years. He had never before expressed his concerns about Pastor Brand that frankly. He was never one to interject himself into my personal life without good reason. Usually, he saw something that I was totally oblivious to, so his comment made me a bit uneasy. I decided to shake off the nerves and turned up the gospel music I had playing. I whispered a prayer in my heart for God's protection from things seen and unseen and put all my worries out of my head.

When I pulled up, Pastor Brand was sitting on his porch. The already thin, dark-skinned man looked even more frail and darker than ever. His cheeks were sunken to the point that he looked ill and his skin seemed lifeless and gray. He had always worn larger and layered clothes to make himself appear less skinny, but they seemed to be hanging off him at this point. He looked as weary as he had stated to me on the phone and even more so now that I was getting a good look at him. At that moment, I was glad to be a refuge during this storm in his life.

Pastor Brand had been married four times previously, and I had watched him through the years enter into relationships that I knew were doomed from the start. His last marriage had been filled with havoc. It was just one moment of drama after another. Though it really caught me off guard when I heard he had married again, I started praying that God would make his marriage strong and that He would use the both of them to do a mighty work for His kingdom.

At first, I prayed for them because it was the Christian thing to do. When I kneeled by my bedside at night and prayed for my loved ones and others the Holy Spirit brought to my remembrance, I would always remember Pastor Brand and his new wife. As time went on, my prayers became more sincere. I wasn't just praying for them because it was the Christian thing to do, but I honestly wanted him to be happy even if it meant me releasing him from my heart.

Pastor Brand and I had developed a true friendship over the years. My first husband and I respected him greatly, and he had been able to reach my husband in a way the pastorship we once sat under had not. My family grew to love and respect him, and he became my spiritual counselor when things started going wrong in my marriage. My then husband had started doing drugs, and with the use of drugs came affair after affair. Eventually, we separated, and he died of cancer two and half years later.

My daughter Sasha respected Pastor Brand, and she was happy I had a good spiritual friend in my life. He would come to our house and do spiritual shut-ins, and I believed our home was blessed because of them. It was good to know that there was a man present in the house although I would see very little of him. Sasha was in high school, and I was taking college classes in addition to being the Saturday morning personality at a local Christian radio station.

The ride back to my home was a silent one. I reflected on the man sitting next to me. The only time he was in my life was when something was going wrong in his. Unbeknownst to me, I had become addicted to being his savior. With me, he could find safety. He could let his guard down completely, and whatever troubles he was running from, he could leave behind. I would heal his wounds, and after getting some rest and a spiritual re-charge, he would disappear as fast as he had come, and my life would go back to normal. I would never have suspected this would be the last call to this stage of my beautifully normal life.

.

CHAPTER FOUR

Beauty For Ashes

It was November 2011, and unspeakable joy in the form of holy matrimony had returned to my life. As I sat in the cushioned chair in the little greeting room, which had now become my dressing room for the day, I found myself wondering if I was making the right decision. The church was decorated in the color scheme of red, black, and white to incorporate the Christmas decorations that were already up at the church. The pews were covered in a bright red, and the carpet in the sanctuary was a peppered red and black. Sister Ruthie, one of the sisters at the church, had offered to decorate for the occasion as a gift for all I had done and meant to the ministry. She had always been supportive of my time spent at Mt. Sharon Missionary Baptist, and when I needed to get a prayer through, she was the sister I would call. If she told you she would be praying with you, she meant just that. She was a Holy Ghost filled pillar in the church.

It was a bittersweet moment for the congregation that had grown to love me. My spiritual father, Pastor Sims, wished me well and had agreed to perform the ceremony. I had been under Pastor Sims' leadership for almost two years and served as one of his associate ministers in the church. He always said I was a breath of freshness because of the change I brought to the ministry. Several visions he had for the church had become a reality, and he welcomed the extra help.

Every first Saturday Pastor Sims and I, along with anyone else who wished, would walk the streets going door to door praying for souls and bringing a word of encouragement to those who were heavy laden. "Taking it to the Streets" became a ministry outreach at Mt. Sharon, and the services started to grow. The church now had a nursing home ministry, and a youth choir that was full of talent no one in the church had previously recognized. My time had been well spent at Mt. Sharon, and I had grown to love them as much as they loved me.

Though Pastor Sims knew very little of Pastor Thomas Brand, he trusted and respected my decision to become his wife, and he knew if we worked together we would be a dynamic team in the ministry.

"You can always come back home if you need to," said Pastor Sims as he looked me directly in the eyes. "I know you are going to be good to him and he better be good to you."

I nodded as I reached to hug him and thank him for his guidance, and for mentoring me for this next chapter in my life.

"We will be fine. If two saints can't make a marriage work what hope is there for the world?" I asked.

Pastor Sims lowered his head to peak over his glasses, which had settled lower on his nose and said, "It is supposed to work that way, but unless Jesus is in a thing it will not work. You know Jesus, and he knows Jesus; be good to each other. I really wish I had sat down with the two of you. I love you."

"Awww, I love you too, and I am going to make

you proud," I replied as I hugged him once again.

Though there were some who felt this union was a grave mistake on my part, I was hearing none of it. I had watched Pastor Brand for years and yes it was true when it came down to marriages and relationships, his track record was not the greatest in the world. But, it would be different with me. He was always better after spending time with me, and I would see to it that our marriage would be the exception to his previous ones.

My family had always told me I was gullible. Let them tell it; I believed whatever people told me. They thought I was too much of an optimist and the reality of a matter is usually something different than what I wanted to believe. They always said I believe there is good in everyone and that I see no evil. The world I live in, according to them, does not exist and not everyone who cries "Lord, Lord" lives the life of a Christian. I guess I did live in a bubble. God had blessed me to come in contact with people who are who they say they are. People who still believe a person's word is his bond and still adopt the concept of loving your neighbor as you love yourself.

It wasn't long after I married Pastor Brand and

became his First Lady that my bubble burst and the reality of my world became the reality of his; a cauldron of ashes. The man in the pulpit was not the man I took home. He could usher me into the presence of the Lord so sweetly but had abandoned me in so many other ways. As my protector, he had become the one inflicting the pain. As my provider, he was the one starving me to death. As the priest of our home, he became my fall from grace. Because of who I was, the First Lady of a growing ministry, I was forced to wear a mask of deception that would eventually terminate everything I stood for. I traded the beauty of my life in Christ for the ashes of a dark heart.

CHAPTER FIVE

The Veil

I sat on the side of my bed wondering how I had gotten to this place where I no longer knew who I was. I had become a puppet whose strings were being pulled by everyone but me. I now wore a mask for every aspect of my life.

My thoughts became consumed with wondering whether this was something all First Ladies experienced but chose to keep hidden. Was this really normal? Did I not understand the life of a pastor's wife? Was the treatment I was receiving from my husband normal for my position? Did I truly not know what I was signing on for when I married a pastor? Was my treatment the cross I was to carry as a First Lady and Co-Pastor?

My heart shook at the thought of such things being true, and I declared with all that was left of me that I would not buy into that ideology. This is not the way it is supposed to be. This is not God's intent for His leaders; the shepherds of His flock. This is not the way things are supposed to be in the ministry. If two people preaching the gospel cannot save their marriage and if two people preaching the gospel cannot be examples for the people, what hope did those couples have who weren't as close to God?

I purposed in my heart that my marriage would not be another blemish to the gospel. My marriage would not be seen as a sign of hopelessness for other married couples who were trying to make it, nor would it be a detour for people who truly wanted to find some truth and safety in the Lord and in the church. I will carry this cross until God fixes things, I thought to myself.

I put on my mask and whispered a prayer as I went out to worship with the congregation. None of them were aware of the fact their First Lady was about to endure one of the many humiliating times of her adult life when days of desperation and pain were unrivaled by the darkest of demonic attacks.

Thomas sat on the front pew. The leader of the "Amen Chorus," he led the people to believe that he was the husband of all husbands. Supposedly supportive in every way, he was the man of God who trusted his pulpit to his bride as much as he trusted her with his life. This, of course, was a totally different tune from what he had stated just minutes before, behind closed doors.

"That Pastor Sims and them folks at Mt. Sharon got to be the most disrespectful folks on the planet! How dare they invite you to preach and overlook me? And you! You had the nerve to accept like you don't have enough to do around here."

Thomas had been in rare form ever since I had gone into consecration the Wednesday before I was to preach for Family & Friends day at my former church. Our ministry had services every Sunday, but this program was in the afternoon, so I accepted. Before a big ministering engagement, I liked to do a lot of meditation, prayer, and reading to be prepared to go before God's people. The service would be held on Sunday at 2:00 pm so I went into meditation the previous Wednesday night after our Bible study. By Friday, he was criticizing me.

He told me I didn't need to be putting all that time

into ministering to someone else's people and not putting in time like that to minister to our people. This was the first time I had seen him act that way. He had known I was a minister when he married me and he knew how much the people at Mt. Sharon loved me. They had all accepted me as their associate minister, and Pastor Sims was an awesome spiritual father.

I stopped studying or meditating at home. I would do it in my car or on my lunch break at work. When the Sunday came for me to travel to Clearville to preach, Thomas held his service longer than usual. To make matters even worse, when service was over, he sent someone to get pizza for everyone before we got on the road. There would be plenty of food served at Mt. Sharon, and yet he acted as if our people could not go four hours without eating.

The program at Mt. Sharon was to start at 2:00 pm and we were just leaving our church at 1:30 pm for an hour trip. On the bright side, our entire congregation was going with us, and that made me very happy. I wanted Pastor Sims to see the progress we had made with our ministry and the people we had won off the streets. Thomas nagged the entire way.

"If you think I'm going to have the people running up and down the road behind you, you have another thing coming. I'm the Pastor, and I am not going to be sitting down in a seat listening to my wife preach!"

It was terrible. I could not believe what I was hearing.

When we arrived at the church, they had already started devotion, and the ushers directed Thomas and me to the pastor's study. Pastor Sims could tell something was wrong, but I tried to play it off, not wanting him to know that my husband was upset. Finally, Thomas asked Pastor Sims if he would give us a minute. Pastor Sims reluctantly left his office saying he was going to check on the sound system.

Thomas actually started in on me again about them asking me to preach and not him. He got so loud that Pastor Sims came back into his study and just sort of stood around. When Thomas left the office, Pastor Sims asked me if everything was okay.

"Yes, Sir," I mumbled, wanting to believe the words I was speaking.

"Normally, I never leave my study like that. I know it is hard, but do what you do. I know you can preach and that is what we are expecting. God got you."

Although Pastor Sims reassured me, I wanted to break down and cry, but I knew I had to keep it together so I could get through the service.

When my husband introduced me that day, it was as if nothing had happened. Once again, I was his loving wife, an awesome woman of God, a woman who could really preach, a woman who had been giving herself to the Lord all week to have a word for the people. He exclaimed how he could not be doing so well with his ministry if I were not by his side. He turned it on and off just like that. I was amazed. In front of people, he treated me so sweetly, but behind closed doors, ninety percent of the time, he was treating me as if I was his worst enemy.

The service was awesome that day. God really moved, and the church was packed. He was the loving, supportive husband during and after the service. As I knew would be the case, Mt. Sharon did have plenty of food for everyone to eat and we stayed and enjoyed the fellowship. The day was ending well after all; or so I thought.

I was staying in Clearville because I had to work that night and Thomas had decided to return to Dobson with the other members of our church. He left without even telling me he was leaving. I looked around, and he was gone. No "great job"; no "see you later"; no goodbye kiss. He just left.

After that incident, I stopped accepting speaking engagements. I would encourage anyone who wanted me to come to preach to ask my husband instead. To this day, he does not know I did that, but it made our home a happier place. After all, he was a really, really good preacher.

That night became like one of many others to come. I wrapped myself in a veil of tears and fell asleep sobbing for the broken me, and wishing for the "me" I once was. All I could do was hold on until morning. God's mercies are new then, and hopefully, I could hope again.

CHAPTER SIX

Still, Small Voice

F or the next several days I wrestled with the enemy. I knew in my heart it had to be him because why else would I be second guessing my marriage? After all, I had seen our future, and we were preaching before thousands and had a national broadcasting ministry. I had seen us traveling to foreign countries and our mission ministry being referred to as a "powerhouse." God had shown me a great work that Thomas and I were going to do together and that our union was going to be a complete turnaround for his life. So I became even more intentional and intense in my nightly prayer.

Once I got Papa and Nana tucked in for the night, I would go into the living room and start some serious praying. I would ask God to open my husband's eyes to see what I saw and to remove any negative influences from his life. I would plead for God to help him recognize the tricks of the devil. I wanted him to see that I loved him and that I was not his enemy. I wanted God to help me be what my husband needed me to be and to not let me lose who I was. I prayed for God to give my husband a double portion of His knowledge, wisdom, and understanding.

I encouraged myself by speaking aloud that, "This time, this ministry will not be destroyed because of his actions. This time it will be different. This time he had me and together we would be great in the ministry". I prayed that prayer for many nights and months. It seemed the more I prayed, the worse it got.

Had my vision been wrong? Were we not destined to be this power couple in the ministry? Did I see something that my husband was not capable of being? How could I have seen it so wrong? How could this be what I had been waiting for all those years and it not be as expected? How could I not see who my husband really was? It went against everything I believed.

I believed that if you are up preaching it, you are living it. You cannot be one person in front of the people and someone totally different otherwise. Everyone preaching the gospel was living it to the best of their ability, and God had chosen them to be a shepherd over His people because of that. Pastors were not deceivers. They were real and feared God with all their hearts.

Was it possible that I was wrong about all of that? Had I been so blind to the reality of this the entire nine years I had been in the ministry? My soul cried out at the thought of this being true, and I decided the answer was emphatically "NO." I had not been blind.

There are some really good pastors and pastors' wives out there. There had to be couples who were living and preaching the gospel under the instruction and fear of God. I had spent the past two years in the presence of many awesome pastors and their wives.

Surely, I could not have been that deceived by Thomas when he asked me to marry him. We had been friends for so many years; it seemed like I knew him inside and out. During his last retreat at my home, I felt like I knew him more than ever. Even though the announcement of his interest in me as more than a friend was a surprise, I felt honored that he came as a man desiring me as his wife and our relationship entered a new level.

Seeing the band on my finger, he believed I was still wearing my wedding band and did not have any problem questioning me about it. I explained to him how God had come to me in my dream and how God and I were married. I also explained to him what God had told me about the man who would remove the band from my finger. I can still see him sighing as he said, "Those are some big shoes to fill."

What he did not know was I believed him to be more than man enough to remove the band, and it was not a coincidence that he had come into my life at that particular time. The chastity band I once wore on my wedding ring finger cracked three months after he and I started spending time together. Though I was still trying to wear it, it completely split in half and was no longer wearable. I took it as a sign from God that Thomas's ring would be my replacement; the right man had finally been sent to fill those big shoes.

A year later, I sat in the greeting room at Mt. Sharon. I had asked myself if I was making the right decision. For that year, Pastor Brand and I seemed happy when we were together. I quickly removed any doubt from my mind and remembered what God had spoken to me and focused on Pastor Brand's tender proposal. But as it typically goes, ignoring that still, small voice was one of the biggest mistakes I would ever make.

CHAPTER SEVEN

Just a Building

When we got married, and at the age of 51, Thomas did not have anything to bring to the table as far as wealth. He was living in pastoral housing, which left a lot to be desired. The oddly painted sky blue apartment complex was run down, and the tenants were mostly the unemployed and those who drew monthly government checks.

Though the complex was owned by a ministry, its occupants were not ministry minded. On any given day, you could hear loud music, profanity, or someone fighting. The grounds were not well kept, and trash was always scattered about. Yet, there was Pastor Brand, living right in the middle of it all. He didn't have a car, and the only income was the $100.00 a week he got paid from the ministry as their full-time pastor. But to me, he was a king. My life was very comfortable, and I was one of those sisters who did not mind helping a brother get on his feet. Working together, I knew we would be able to accomplish anything.

Life was good. We commuted between our two homes, and he would always have his apartment clean and dinner ready when he knew I was coming home. We spent our nights watching movies and laughing about funny stuff that had happened during the day. It was time well spent, and when he took me in his arms at night and made passionate love to me, any problems I had faced during the day disappeared.

"We really need to get you a car," I said as Thomas opened the door of my vehicle to get inside. "If you had a car, you could already be at the house in Clearville when I get off, and we would have more time to spend together."

"I know, and I do like getting away from this apartment complex sometimes. I want to spend more time at our home, but I am unable to get there unless you pick me up. If I get someone to bring me, they all want gas money, and I do not have any money," Thomas said, sounding aggravated.

Wanting him to feel less dependent on others, including myself, I reached over and propped my hand on his leg as I always did when we were traveling and said, "Next week we will start looking for you a vehicle."

Two weeks later, I purchased Thomas a car. It made it easier for him to get around and he was happy to know that I did not have to be on the road so much. He could now come to me instead of me having to pick him up all the time. It made me happy that he had a sense of independence. It was also nice when I got off on Fridays, to have my husband at the house anxiously awaiting my arrival.

That's why I was totally unprepared for what happened next.

"Well, the get together was about me, and I am no longer the pastor under Bishop." Thomas dropped this bomb on me as I entered his apartment several months into our marriage.

"What are you talking about?" He could tell that I

was clearly confused. "What meeting? I thought you said you were not going to the get-together?"

"They kept calling me, and I went, but if I had known it was a meeting about me, I would not have gone. They were all there from the church, including Bishop, and they all had something negative to say about me. If you had been there as my wife they would not have handled me that way," Thomas said, blaming me.

"You said it was a get-together and the last thing you told me was you were not going."

"I am no longer the pastor under Bishop, and the get together was really a meeting about me," he repeated again. This time though his tone was more hostile.

Not really knowing what to say, I sat there in awe wondering why the church had decided to dismiss him so abruptly and why I was somehow being blamed for the events that had taken place. I tried to encourage him, to let him know God had a plan and everything would be okay. He simply gave me a cold look and ignored me. We spent the night in silence.

I later found out there had been some questioning of his behavior as a pastor and the relationship was severed. Though I did not know the exact details of his release, I believe his time at this church had run its course, and it was time for him to focus on what God had for him to do next. I would just have to assure him that I would be there no matter what.

A month later, we were having church services in the conference room of a local bank, and things were off to a good start. My husband had the ability to build a church, but his problem was keeping one going once he got it started. Our congregation consisted of people off the streets or people who were not going to church anywhere. There were no recycled Christians from other churches. Thomas and I were a team and had each other's back.

We did have one awesome family who had joined us from Beyond the Jordan Ministries, the Mason family, and they were very influential in helping us get the ministry off the ground. They had a lot of respect for my husband, and I quickly grew to love and respect them. When he was released from his position at Beyond the Jordan Ministries, he also lost clergy housing and was staying in Dobson with his daughter and her family because of work. Luckily, he'd at least gotten a job once he got a car. On the weekends he would come to

Clearville and spend time at our home, but once we started the ministry, those visits became far and few between and sometimes the only time we would be in the same room was on Sundays. I did not like our current situation, but it was a sacrifice I was willing to make for the sake of the gospel. He would always tell me things would get better soon and to give him a little more time to get things in order. Our time spent together was time well spent and I believed that he was really trying.

Unfortunately, things only got tougher as time went on. I started making excuses for how he treated me. I blamed it on the enemy trying to keep us from becoming that power couple in the ministry. Although the congregation was growing, our love was not. I soon came to see that no ministry was worth its salt in the earth if it didn't have love between the shepherds and love for the people. It was just a building.

CHAPTER EIGHT

White Flags

There have been times in my life where I could count on discernment to make all the difference and keep me from dangers, seen and unseen. I could think deeply about something and learn from the Holy Spirit that it was definitely not a good idea. It was a safeguard against my so-called gullible nature, and it helped me build a life of peace and one with no regrets. I became pretty good at seeing red flags and avoiding disaster. Yet, I learned that love can blind you to discernment and hush the voice of the Holy Spirit.

It was Valentine's week, and everyone at the

church was excited. Thomas was in good spirits, and this was the second Valentine's Day we would spend together since we got married. Things were looking up. We were settled in our new church building, and the ministry was growing. He was really good at coming up with different activities to give the people something else to do on occasions like this. This year, he was putting together a Valentine's Ball.

Everyone was excited and had purchased their tickets. I had not seen how he had decorated the church because I had been working night and day all week and had not been to the church. I was so amazed when I walked in the sanctuary. It was breathtaking! He had done a great job transforming the room into a romantic setting and had picked the perfect colors and décor.

What really made me feel we were back on the right track was the fact that he had set up a table just for us; he had balloons, flowers, and a teddy bear waiting at the table for me. I was overwhelmed with joy; this was the man I married. The man I had not seen enough of lately, but I was glad I was seeing him that night. To make things even better, he sang to me in front of everyone.

"The question is, will I ever leave you and the answer is no, no, no, no, no, no-noooo-nooo-no, no," he crooned. Everyone was clapping and cheering as I gave him a passionate kiss when he finished. He was actually blushing. This was the man I fell in love with. Needless to say, the rest of the night was magical. He made me feel like I was the only woman on the face of the earth as he stroked my hair with his hands while looking into my eyes. He told me I was so beautiful and he was sorry for the way he had been acting. I believed him because I felt at that moment he meant every word. It was a welcome change from what had become a bottomless pit of sacrifice.

I had been carrying the load when Thomas got released as pastor from Beyond the Jordan Ministries. He had no income, so he moved into our home in Clearville. I paid for everything. I gave him money so he would not be broke. While I worked each day, he would go job hunting or out to minister. At least that is what he told me he was doing. Whatever he was up to, he eventually got a job as a welder.

We looked at our finances and said we were going to pool our money together so we could really do some things. Once he started working, all that changed. I had to ask for the $100.00 a week he said he was going to give me to help take care of household expenses. Eventually, I stopped asking because it would always end with him being distant towards me. I figured as long as he was making payments on the vehicle I had purchased for him in my name, I would be okay with that.

We went out to lunch one Saturday at a restaurant that he really liked, but I didn't care for the menu items that much. Because I knew he really liked the restaurant, I did not say anything, and I managed to find a decent soup to order. I no longer felt comfortable eating around him since he had made it clear how he felt about my size. Once we had finished eating, our waitress brought us the check. Since he picked up the check, I left the tip on the table. I had no reason to think he would have a problem with this. What happened next cut like a two edge sword and I was the receiver.

When we got outside to get in the vehicle, he said, "If you think that because I am working I am going to spend all my money on you and be paying when we go out to eat you got another thing coming." I was shocked! He wasn't paying any bills in our home. He was barely giving me the money for his car payment, and I was paying all of the auto insurance for both his vehicle and mine. Again, I could not believe what I was hearing. He was so cold when he said it. I could not help but wonder what he was doing with his money.

The real wonder came when I had to make the most humiliating phone call of my life.

"Hey Sasha."

"Hi, Mom. What's up?"

"Hey listen, don't worry when I ask you what I'm about to ask and please don't ask any questions because it's hard enough for me." I could hear the catch in her throat when she mouthed back, "Okay."

"I need to borrow $200.00 for our car insurance. Will you loan it to me until I get paid?"

Sasha was speechless. Never had she heard me ask for money. She was used to me being the one lending instead of borrowing. She was used to me being the strong one. The one who always had it together spiritually and financially. I felt crushed at the thought of what she must be feeling in that moment. I tried to lighten things up and reassure her it was a temporary thing and it was nothing but a glitch in the finances.

When she said yes I was relieved and ashamed all at once. I knew she would keep it between us. Although I could've gone to Mr. Miller or other friends I knew, it was just too embarrassing. I didn't want to be the First Lady out begging. Sasha had saved what little bit of public dignity I had left.

I asked her to transfer the money to my bank account. I didn't tell her it was because I was too embarrassed to make the exchange from her hand to mine when I was so accustomed to it being the other way around. When I hung up the phone, I realized that all the red flags that God had been giving me along the way I'd been painting white. Surrendering a little piece of my soul and all of my peace with each one. I took a deep breath, thanked God for my baby girl, and put my mask on as I went in to work.

CHAPTER NINE

Back to Beautiful

I was a curvy woman, definitely no size two, but because of my height I carried my weight very well and I was always seen as pretty. Friends would remark on how my smile lit up the room and my previous husband said my eyes could draw anyone into my web. My height and size were always comfortable to me and comforting to those I embraced.

I dressed very modestly to make sure any revealing flesh was appropriate. I did not like men gawking at me. My legs were long and shapely, the one thing I had gotten from my biological family that I loved, and when I put on stilettos, my cocoa colored legs were even the more inviting. Shoulder length and jet black, my hair was usually pulled back or pinned up because I didn't like the feel of hair on my face or neck. Generally, I wouldn't be what people would consider outspoken, although I could be when it mattered. I was more soft-spoken and observant. I had learned the less said, the better until a person had really studied their surroundings. The way I stood, walked and talked announced my professionalism, and I had the ability to bring excitement to any conversation. I felt as though I really displayed that I was a woman of God with excellence and grace despite my size. My big was beautiful.

We had completed one of our Wednesday night services, and instead of going home, I decided to stay the night at the church with my husband since I had to get up early for work the next day. He was more distant than usual that night in service, and I felt a little rejected by him. He had been staying at the church because he said he had to be there more in order to build the ministry; plus, he was working and wanted to be close to the job site.

"I don't like big women," Thomas said coldly, as I

undressed for bed that night.

I could not understand how he could be making a big deal about my size since I was now smaller than I was the day we got married. Besides, even if I was the same size as when we got married, it was never an issue before so why would it be an issue now? Who are you looking at that now makes me undesirable because of my size? I told him that if he was really concerned about my weight, we could fix that. I could lose the weight. He just put his hands in his pocket and started walking back and forth in his office. He said it would help and I assured him I would lose the weight.

He looked at me as if he was disappointed in my answer, sat down in his chair, and started rubbing his forehead with the palm of his hands.

I said, "See, it did not fix anything did it?"

"Let's just go to bed."

I stayed in the office to let out the sofa bed as Thomas left to go to the bathroom. It was a while before I noticed he had not returned. I walked into the hallway and heard him in the bathroom on his cellphone. I knocked on the door and asked him who he was talking to. When he did not answer, I returned to the office. I knew he was on the phone with a woman because I heard her voice.

When he came out the bathroom, he said, "This is not working for me."

"What's not working for you?"

"I am not happy."

"Who were you on the phone with?"

"Pastor Rob. I was telling him how I feel and he said I should be honest with you."

"A pastor is telling you to end a marriage you have only been in for six months instead of telling you to tough it out?

I went to sleep after crying inside. He would normally cuddle up next to me, but this particular night he made sure he did not touch me at all in bed. My female intuitions were working overtime and I knew he had made plans to be with someone else but he had no idea I would be staying at the church that night. He had no idea I had taken off from my night job so I could spend some time with him. In other words, I was a hindrance to what he wanted to do and who he wanted to do it with.

I thought to myself, how was it possible for a man

to make plans to cheat on his wife and treat her like an inconvenience for wanting to spend time with him? Why even think it's okay to take it out on her because your mistress is angry? I am the wife. How are you going to make some other woman more important than your wife? If I had known Thomas was still interacting with his ex-wife, I would not have married him.

It was Mother's Day, and our service was full. We knew we had to start looking for a larger location. In no time the bank conference room would not be able to hold the attendance we were getting every Sunday.

The opening of the service was a bit of a struggle that Sunday but things quickly changed once my husband got up to preach. He recognized all the mothers in the church and encouraged all the men to treat the mothers special and to make sure that today was their day. I was ecstatic. Since he had started working, I was seldom able to see him, and it was so good knowing the two of us was going to spend some quality time together after the service.

I always sat on the front row to support my husband, so I did not see the devil appear in the service. Yet there she was sitting right in the middle of our congregation seducing my husband with the sound of a tambourine. I noticed Thomas's countenance change, and then his message lost its meaning. I no longer felt his spirit tugging on mine, and his message was exceptionally short that day.

After the service, I expected him to tell me what he had planned for me, but when I approached him, he was agitated and spoke coldly to me.

"I only have one day off to do what I want to do, and I am not going to spend my only day off with you," he said as he walked towards the car I had purchased for him several months earlier.

I got in the car puzzled, unable to believe my husband was talking to me so rudely. It was as if another spirit had taken him over and it did not like being in my presence. Realizing something was seriously wrong with him and wanting to follow peace, I looked at him and said, "You were the one saying you were going to make this day special for me, if you do not want to do anything with me you do not have to and if you are going to be ugly to me, I would prefer you didn't do anything with me."

He quickly agreed to that suggestion, and I called

my sister to meet us so I could catch a ride home with her. I was so embarrassed for her to know that he was not taking me out to lunch or doing anything with me. She too knew that we had been spending little time together since starting the church and although she did not understand it, she accepted my understanding of it and did not press the issue.

He dropped me off in the parking lot and drove off without so much as a goodbye. I tried to hold back the tears, not wanting my sister to know there was something wrong, but her sisterly instincts kicked in.

"Where is Thomas going? Is he not spending time with you today?"

As I shook my head no, the tears started rolling down my face, and she started shaking her head in anger.

"Who was the woman that walked into the service, the one he kept walking by and touching on the shoulder?"

I had no idea that had even happened, but when she described her to me, I knew exactly who she was. Thomas's ex-wife had shown up at our service that day, and for some reason it caused him to act out. His whole message was off once she had entered the sanctuary and his treatment of me had quickly changed.

I learned so much that day. I learned that shame and regret come in the form of feeling inadequate. Feeling unappreciated makes us look to the one who claims to love us most for our beauty. It got to the point that my beauty was no longer enough to me, so when the devil showed up at church, she had already replaced the beauty Thomas once saw in me.

I had forgotten that beauty is as beauty does and I no longer displayed the excellence and grace of God's daughter from the inside. Sure, on the outside, it was there, but Thomas knew me. He knew the compromises I had made for him, and it made me unattractive to him. He needed someone who could be his equal to his evil and he knew I could not be that woman.

I didn't know what to do from there, but this I did know: I would find my way back from the hurt of this Mother's Day. I would find my way back from that phone call in the bathroom. I would find my way back to beautiful.

PART 2
The Church Ladies Speak

CHAPTER TEN

LaTicia

"A re you okay, First Lady?" I asked as I helped her up from the floor.

"I am fine. All is well," she answered as she took hold of my arm to pull herself up.

Her hazel brown eyes were outlined blood red and the tears flowing down her cheeks were a stream of black mascara. As she tried to pull herself together and get ready to go out and minister to the people, I stood there looking at her. I could tell she would not be able to endure the treatment she was receiving from Pastor much longer.

As her trusted armor bearer, I had witnessed his treatment of her for quite some time, but she always tried to cover up for him. Many of us in the congregation wondered why she continued to tolerate his treatment, but we knew First Lady was real with her walk with Christ, which meant she would not be one to walk away unless things became intolerable. Being the praying woman she was, I knew that could take some time.

"I am so sorry First Lady," I said as I helped her zip her robe.

"All is well, LaTicia," she replied again as she walked over to the mirror hanging on the entrance door to the sanctuary. "All is well."

Wiping the tears from her eyes and mascara from her face, she cleared her throat and asked how I was doing.

"I am doing fine," I replied. "What would you like to drink today?"

"A bottle of cold water will be fine," she sighed as she pushed her hair behind her ears.

I could hear Pastor opening up the service as he started playing the keyboard. Pastor had given First Lady the second Sunday to minister to the people, but he always managed to upset her meditation time. It was as if he was setting her up to fail by distracting her so she would not be able to put her best foot forward.

"Well, shall we pray?" she asked as she cleared her throat.

I looked forward to this moment every second Sunday because I could feel the presence of the Lord enter the room every time she prayed before going out to the sanctuary.

"Yes, Ma'am. I am so ready."

"Me too."

As we joined hands, the ranting Pastor had done previously became a distant memory, and she was entering that zone. Everyone and everything was tuned out except for God, and her mind was focused on the Lord and Him moving in the service.

"God, we come before You humbly asking You to forgive us of our sins and turn Your ears to our prayer. Move in the service today. Speak to Your people as only You can. Decrease me and increase Your spirit within me. God, touch my husband this morning. Give him a double portion of Your wisdom, knowledge, and understanding. Teach him to love me and be the husband that you are calling him to be. Help us to remember when we first fell in love. Lord, we are expecting a great move of Your Holy Spirit this morning. Let Your anointing fall in this place. Mend broken hearts, heal marriages, save the unsaved, and bring about realness in your people in Jesus' name. Amen." she prayed.

I squeezed her hands once again to let her know I was in agreement with her on the request for which she was petitioning God and then we embraced.

Rumors had started swirling around that Pastor was having an affair, but I could tell that the First Lady had not gotten wind of it yet. To her, he was the greatest husband in the world. I truly do not understand how she came to that conclusion. He was in his early fifties and did not have anything material to show for his time spent on this earth. He had started two other ministries prior to this one, and they had failed due to his lack of commitment to the word he was teaching. He preaches and teaches the Bible, but it was evident that he was unable to live it. No matter how his congregation grew, he still could not get beyond a storefront church, and his best people always ended up leaving once they saw his imperfections and experienced his ranting.

As her armor bearer, I would go into prayer every Saturday night before the second Sunday asking God to bridle Pastor's mouth. It didn't seem to work, but I prayed anyway. I can still hear him yelling at her as I stood outside his office door.

"God made me the pastor of these people. You are always taking up for them, but you do not have to deal with them like I do," he said.

"I am not saying that God did not make you the pastor of these people, I am just saying you can't yell and belittle people because they are not doing what you think they should do. You are going to run some of our best people away."

"I do not care! They can go and so can you!" He yelled right before he told her not to say another word. The room became silent for a minute, and then he started ranting again. "For you to be so smart you are stupid. That is why you can't let people preach; they start getting the big head, thinking they know more than the pastor."

As the door swiftly swung open, catching me off guard, I tried to pretend I had not heard the conversation that had taken place on the other side of the door.

"Good morning, Sister. So glad to see you," he

said with a big smile on his face as he put his arm around me to greet me with a hug.

"Good morning, Pastor," I forced myself to say as my eyes searched for First Lady.

Once he walked down the hallway, I entered the office, and she was sitting at his desk with her head down as if she was so focused on reading the Word, but I knew her well enough to know she was trying to make sure I did not see the tears running down her face.

The first time I witnessed this, it literally broke my heart. I was excited that Pastor had appointed me as armor bearer and I was on my post. I went to stand by the front door and waited to be called in to help First Lady with whatever she needed.

Then, the door slammed open. It was First Lady with her Bible in her hand, and her robe half zipped. Shaking her head, she looked at me and said, "I will be right back." I knew she was trying to get away from Pastor.

As I walked into his office, he was sitting at his desk with a look of victory on his face. I tried to seem ignorant to what may have happened, but I had a questioning look on my face. I wanted to, in some way, help him understand the hurt and confusion that permeated the room. It was to no avail. That demon was strong and determined to stay in control. I dropped my head and went to the bathroom to check on First Lady.

First Lady was easy to care for and assist. She always had a smile on her face and a motherly, nurturing spirit about her. She could be having the worse of the worst days, and she always found a way to make someone else smile. This is why it was so hard for people to tell her about the rumors that Pastor was cheating. I for one didn't want to be the one to hurt her like that; I just couldn't think of doing such a thing. I would just wait. God always had a way of pointing out wolves in sheep's clothing. I would just be there to help her pick up the pieces when it did finally come to light.

CHAPTER ELEVEN

Sadie

My name Bennett and I ain't it!" I laughed as I took another bite of food. Some of the other members were whispering amongst themselves about how pastor was playing games. They said it had been messy of him to order pizza when he knew First Lady had to go preach.

"Y'all know y'all happy to have this pizza and you gonna be happy to eat whatever they have at the other church so stop playing," I continued. "I don't even know why y'all in these folks business. First Lady gonna do what she gotta do anyways."

I hated hearing them talk about Pastor and First

Lady. It boiled my grits! Folks were always in each other's business, but couldn't get their own lives straight. I told them they need to start praying more and talking less. Then I sent one of the children to get me two more slices of pizza.

I looked over at First Lady and could see that she was trying to hold it together. She was always so graceful. She carried herself my like sister, Mattie. The only difference was Mattie always wore hats and gloves on Sundays. Other than that, they were a lot alike. I guess that's why I loved First Lady so much.

I loved Pastor too. I didn't like how he treated First Lady, but I knew he could really get a word from the Lord to give to us when we needed it most. I knew he couldn't be all bad if God would use him to bless us. Besides, First Lady was the best thing to happen to him in a long time. I had heard the rumors about him cheating on her, but you would never catch me repeating that mess. I told everybody who came to me with it to tell her themselves. He wasn't my husband, so it wasn't my concern. That would hush them up from coming to me.

I always invited First Lady over to my apartment for Jamaican food. She seemed to love it more than me. It was a chance for her to have a break. I liked having her there and making her laugh. She was like Mattie, she would laugh all prissy like, but you knew she loved a good joke. If she opened up about Pastor, I listened but I never brought it up, and I never uttered a bad word about the man of God. I just listened because I knew she had very few people she could talk to about what was going on with her and Pastor. Either way, she would only talk for a few minutes and then get right back to making me cut up and act silly.

When we got to Mt. Sharon for First Lady to preach that day, I could tell she was a little anxious about us being late. But God blessed her and, as always, she delivered a fine sermon. No one could even tell that Pastor had given her his usual hard time before she preached. As a matter of fact, when he introduced her, you'd have thought she was Woman of the Year and he was the most loving husband in the world.

I told First Lady that day to not ever stop preaching. God has a word inside of her that can't no devil stop unless she lets him. I prayed for her right then and there. I felt the Spirit move, and we had church right there in that corner. Laughing, we entered the fellowship hall. I had worked up an appetite with all that praying.

That was the last time I really got to spend time with First Lady one-on-one. Shortly after that, the devil came to church with her tambourine and the little light First Lady had left began to dim. She became more closed off and although she was sweet as ever, she wasn't as open as she was before.

I didn't take it personally like some of the other folks. Besides, I knew they were listening to Pastor tell them things about her that weren't true. He was making her look bad and getting them to think she had a Jezebel spirit, and wanted to destroy the ministry to start her own church. That really broke my heart because I really looked up to Pastor. I couldn't believe he would ruin her name all the while he was messing around. It just made me pray harder for First Lady, and I kept inviting her over just so she knew she had someone there who cared.

CHAPTER TWELVE

Jerica

D addy, I'm leaving the house now."
"You late on the one day I need you here!"
"I know; I told you Jordan had to work late last night. He had to get some sleep so he could be alert to take care of the kids while I'm gone."

"I ain't worried about that. Just get here!"

Daddy always had a way of making me feel like a mistake. I could never do anything to please him. It seems like he and my half-sister get along great. He watches her kids, goes places with her, and cuts her all kinds of slack when she is late or doesn't show up at all. Then he acts like I should be happy to fill in for her when she's not there to usher when she's supposed to. Sometimes, I would have to usher two weeks in a row. I just want him to see how hard I'm trying to please him.

I can't wait to get to the L.I.I.F.T meeting this week. It was even better than Wednesdays because we got to really talk about what was on our hearts. I really liked that name, **L**adies **I**ncreasing **I**n **F**aith **T**ogether, because that's what I was trying to do. When First Lady started the ministry a lot of us were kind of shy about opening up, but once we saw how she just listened to us without judging and then gave real advice we could use, we found it was easier to talk than to suffer in silence.

We all knew about the things First Lady was going through with my dad. I could hardly stand it, but I didn't speak to him about it because I didn't want to hurt my chances of my dad loving me more. We all stayed hush-hush about it. I wonder why? I wonder why none of the sisters her age ever told her what my daddy was doing?

I prayed hard for First Lady. I also made sure whenever she preached on second Sundays, I was there on time and dressed up nice for the praise team so I could really help her do her best. All that fussing Daddy did before it was time for her to preach made me feel even more sorry for her. She just kept on getting up and bringing a sure word.

"It's about time you got here! Go get the mics ready." Daddy scowled and looked me up and down as I sat in the car, ripped from my thoughts as I pulled up to the church.

"Yes, Sir." I just hung my head, didn't make eye contact and went to the sound room.

"You okay, Hun?"

"Yes, First Lady. I'm just gonna get these mics ready, and I'll be right out."

"Take your time, Sister Jerica. The people have barely started coming in."

That was First Lady; always thoughtful and patient. I never saw her one time make a bad face or say anything negative. I couldn't understand why my dad was so mean to her.

I always wanted to call First Lady mom, but I didn't know how Sasha would feel about that. I remember once I asked my dad what he thought about it and he said coldly, "Why you gonna put yourself through that? She ain't gonna be around long enough for it to matter." My heart stopped in my chest. It was all I could do to hold back the tears. He was throwing away the best thing that ever happened to him for that greasy old woman that nobody liked. I hated to hear her tambourine. It sounded like something off a Christmas song and made me stop listening to Christmas carols.

Our next L.I.I.F.T meeting was better than I had hoped for. It was cleansing. First Lady used the pain she was going through to help us understand that we could face anything with God. She never spoke any details about her and Daddy, but I could tell that her helping us was helping her. I prayed really hard for her that night. Whether she stayed with Daddy or not, I just wanted her to be happy.

CHAPTER THIRTEEN

Lifted

LaTicia pulled up to the restaurant early for the meeting. She was hoping Jerica would be there. They had gotten kind of close since she started coming to her dad's church. She was glad that they were meeting at a different place this time. Things had not been the same at the church since all the mess between Pastor and First Lady started. Besides, she heard Pastor tell First Lady that he didn't want her having her Jezebel meetings at his church. LaTicia was just glad First Lady didn't stop holding the meetings altogether.

Jerica was relieved when she saw LaTicia pull up.

It was always better when LaTicia was there because they were closer in age than the other ladies and she always helped her get her words out better. It was almost as if LaTicia was waiting to say exactly what Jerica said so they ended up finishing each other's sentences. She walked over to LaTicia's car with a smile.

"Hey, girl!"

"Hey J! I didn't know if you were going to make it."

"Girl, yes. Jordan said he'd watch the kids for me since he is off tonight so I ran out the house real quick before he changed his mind." They laughed and hugged.

They walked into the restaurant complimenting each other on their outfits. As they were being led to the table by a hostess, they noticed Sadie making her way to the restroom. After taking their seats and placing drink orders, they also noticed that First Lady had not yet arrived and began wondering where she could be.

First Lady had called Sadie to let her know she would be late. Someone hit a deer on the two-lane road leading into town, and she would have to wait for them to clear the wreck. She asked Sadie to have the group to pray and order their food. Sadie hung up and waited for the rest of the ladies to arrive. In the meantime, she took advantage of the time to go to the restroom. Because of her weight, she needed all the time she could get.

Soon, Yvonne and Tori arrived. They greeted everyone, and all the woman picked up their menus. Each woman took a moment to bury her face in the menu options. It took a quick minute to get over the nerves of what was about to come. Sharing and revealing intimate details of their lives was new to them. It wasn't like they never called their girlfriends to vent, but this was different.

At L.I.I.F.T, they not only talked about their circumstances, but they also talked about how to deal with them and how God viewed things. It was the only time they could be heard as more than loud and angry, or worse, not heard at all. It was the only time, other than after a good sermon; they felt lifted.

CHAPTER
FOURTEEN
Unbroken

"Oh, y'all made it!" Sadie exclaimed as she wobbled back towards the table. "Chile I had to go the restroom. I had two glasses of tea waiting on y'all to get here. I'm glad y'all got here because I almost ate all the chips and salsa too." She laughed with the other ladies who looked at the remnants of what used to be chips and salsa. "First Lady gonna be a little late but we gon' wait a few minutes to see if anyone else is coming before we get started."

Tori motioned for the server to come over and take her order for more appetizers. She looked at Sadie with a firm look and said, "Now you know ain't nobody else coming. These ol' messy folks ain't trying to come here."

"Girl, stop it. You don't know that for sure. Even if they don't come, we don't know why." Yvonne lightly chastised.

"I don't care what y'all say. It don't make no sense how things been going, and it makes even less sense that folks believe anything bad about First Lady." Tori remarked.

"Tori, you need to learn to look on the bright side. This is a good group of ladies, and I think it's a fine number of us here considering." Sadie said as she asked the server for more tea when he dropped off Tori's chips.

"Well, you know what? Say what you want to, but I think it's a shame."

Yvonne spoke up, "What do you all think is going on in First Lady's head though? I mean, how do you all think she feels?"

"Well, as her armor bearer I can tell you she's really strong. Some of the things she deals with I know I couldn't, but I know it hurts her. She just does a good job at hiding it I think. Either way though, I know she's going to come out on the other side of it unbroken."

"Yeah, I believe that. I just wish there was something we do could besides pray. I feel so helpless watching her and Pastor go through this. Well, we can't go to Pastor because that never turns out good. No matter what, he's always right."

A chorus of agreement rounded the table as the women looked blankly into the air waiting on the next person to speak.

"Well, my name Paul and that's between y'all. I'm just here to love on First Lady and eat. I ain't worried about all that other stuff." Sadie laughed as she snatched her hand back after being tapped by Tori for reaching for a chip.

Everyone laughed out loud. Then Sadie opened with prayer and led the group in scriptures.

CHAPTER FIFTEEN

Seasons

Hello, everyone. I'm so sorry I'm late. You guys know that's unlike me, but this poor guy hit a deer. I'm glad the Lord spared him. How are you all?"

The ladies had just finished their second round of scriptures when First Lady walked in. They were all so happy to see her. She was just as well dressed and all smiles as she'd always been.

"Fine. We're all doing fine," they chimed.

"Good. I know you all have prayed already but I'll just say a quick prayer, and we can get started."

After the prayer, First Lady looked up with a soft but serious look on her face. It was evident that she had come to the table with a full plate, ready to serve. All the ladies unconsciously held their breath waiting to hear what was coming.

First Lady opened her Bible. "I want to read you all something. I know it's something you've all read before, but I want you to close your eyes and really listen and think about what you hear."

To every thing there is a season and a time to every purpose under the heaven:

a time to be born, and a time to die; a time to plant, and a time to pluck up that which is planted;

a time to kill, and a time to heal; a time to break down, and a time to build up;

a time to weep, and a time to laugh; a time to mourn, and a time to dance;

a time to cast away stones, and a time to gather stones together; a time to embrace, and a time to refrain from embracing;

a time to get, and a time to lose; a time to keep, and a time to cast away;

*a time to rend, and a time to sew; a time to keep
silent, and a time to speak;*

*a time to love, and a time to hate; a time of war,
and a time of peace.*

"Jerica, let's start with you. What were you
thinking about when you were hearing this?

"Well," Jerica took a deep breath and sighed
heavily as she tried to formulate her words while holding
back tears. "I think about my dad. I've wondered all this
time why it seems so hard for him to show me love like
he does my sister. I don't know. It talked about a time to
embrace and a time to refrain from embracing. I guess
it's just not time for it, or maybe he never had that time
so he doesn't even know how. I don't know. I guess I just
have to wait it out."

"I can understand that, Jerica. That's good that you
recognize maybe he never had that time. It means you
know a person can't give what they don't have. Maybe
that's a place where you can start to talk to your dad.
Maybe talk to him about how he grew up. It could open a
door for him to share some memories with you that might
help you understand why it is so hard for him to connect
with you the way you desire him too. It might be a good

idea for you to think of him as a friend for now, but respect him as your father. What do you think?"

Jerica's eyes lit up. "Yes. I never thought about that. I always wanted him just to know how to be my dad. Maybe I *can* start to see him as a friend and start with that!" Excitement settled in as she imagined having a true friendship with her dad.

"Good." First Lady reached over and touched Jerica on the hand. "Okay LaTicia, what about you? What did you think about?"

"Oh wow, I'm not even sure if I want to share it."

"It's totally up to you, but I think it would help you and the group if it's so important that you're concerned about it."

"I'll have to think about it a bit more. Can you come back to me?"

"Sure." She nodded. "Okay, Yvonne. How about you?"

"I actually thought about my husband overseas. I've been a military wife for eleven years now. Lately, every time Mike and I get on Skype or talk or whatever, we always end up fighting. I don't want to fight anymore. That last verse really struck me. 'There's a time to love and a time to hate and time of war and a time of peace.' I wonder how Mike feels being away at war, and every time we talk he has to go to war with me again and again. It's like our marriage has turned into some kind of battleground." Yvonne looked up in the air, searching for her next thought. "Would it be too crazy to believe that we can change seasons? Like, I know it says there's a time for everything, but if some things aren't changing like the seasons should, can we do something to make it change? I'm so tired of fighting. Plus, it does no good for me to pray for my husband's safety and then he has to walk into a minefield every time we get a chance to talk."

"I think you answered your own question. The seasons of our lives change because our circumstances change. We just sometimes don't realize we have control over most of our circumstances. Things like how you relate to Mike is a changeable circumstance. You can start by always remembering that you never know when will be the last time you talk to him. We can all remember that. You never want to end a conversation with someone you love with angry words. Talk to Mike about what you learned here. Tell him about the revelation you had. You two will have to work together on it for it to work, but you *can* end the war and have that time of peace."

Unaware that she was doing so, Yvonne put her hands on her heart. Inside, she felt like she needed to cover her heart with grace. The thought of her marriage being renewed and full of hope filled her up. The emptiness was subsiding; she dared to smile and dream about a better love with Mike. "Thank you, First Lady. I will."

First Lady smiled tenderly and nodded. Turning to Tori, she said, "Alright Tori, your turn. What's on your mind?"

"I don't know First Lady, it seemed like all of it was hitting me. I mean, I done been through so much. I get all these men, and none of 'em stay around long. I try to show them so much love. I cook and clean and all that, but they just come and go. I know you tell me all the time I need to take my time and learn how to be by myself, but I just can't seem to do that. When you read the part that says, 'A time to break down and time to build up,' I felt that. At least I felt the breakdown part. I'm just waiting for the building up part."

"Tori, breaking down and building up takes place

at the same time if you break down with the intention to build up. See, when you don't give yourself time to rebuild after a breakup, you end up inviting more destruction because you never took the time or had it in mind to build something newer and better in its place. That's why I keep stressing to you to take some time for yourself. If you build you up enough, no matter what happens with a man, you won't break into pieces or go looking for the next one to fix you. You might be a little battered and bruised; you might even be a little scared. But, you've built something indestructible. Ask God to help you start seeing yourself and loving yourself as the woman you really want to be. When you start to see yourself as someone who not only gives love but also deserves love in return, then you'll know what it means to build up."

"Oh, I never thought about it like that. Well, I guess I can start doing that now because I already know Tyrone getting ready to move and he ain't even said nothing." Tori looked off to the side and stared out the window.

First Lady knew she was at her shut down point and moved on to Sadie. "Sadie, what's on your heart after what we read?"

"My name Clyde and I'ma let it ride!" Sadie laughed heartily and put her hand back into the bowl of chips and salsa. A chorus of laughter erupted once more. It was good to break up the vibe a bit. They all knew Sadie didn't talk about her feelings. "Y'all know I come here, so I'll know what to pray for y'all about. It ain't about me. My sisters need prayer, and I got plenty of those to go around."

First Lady smiled and turned back to LaTicia. "You ready, Sis?"

"Honestly, I'm really afraid to say it. I don't want to hurt anyone's feelings." LaTicia had a look of distress on her face that First Lady hadn't seen before. She felt it was important that she got LaTicia to open up because she didn't want her going home with a heavy heart.

"It's okay, Hun. You can share whatever it is. God knows what we all need, and He will protect our feelings, even if they get hurt they can heal in truth."

LaTicia kept her head down as she began to talk in a slow and muffled tone. "I was thinking about you, First Lady. I thought about that part where it said 'A time to get, and a time to lose; a time to keep, and a time to cast away.' It made me wonder how long you were going to let Pastor treat you so bad." She kept her head down as she heard very subtle gasps from the other ladies at the table.

First Lady sat silently; dumbfounded, struggling to stay poised. Her face flushed with heat as embarrassment set in. She remembered to control her breathing and think before she spoke. She asked the Holy Spirit to keep her in the moment and bless her to hear and to understand, not just react. She gathered her thoughts and turned her eyes to all the ladies who were now staring at her, except LaTicia who still had her head down. First Lady could see they were eagerly awaiting her answer.

"LaTicia, thank you for that. I appreciate your honesty. I know it must have been hard for you to ask that and it is a fair question. You've been by my side through much of this, and you have seen and heard things that most people did not. With that said, yes, you have the right to know why things are the way they are.

First Lady took a deep breath. "The truth is, I have to stay until God tells me to leave. I don't know how that's going to look, how He's going to say it, but I will know when the time comes. I can't give up on my marriage because it's hard. I can't give up on my husband because he's not what I want him to be. It will have to be God who says when it's too much. Until then, I just have to rely on His strength and hold it together.

Ladies, I'm just like you all. I'm waiting for this season to pass. I know I told Yvonne that she can change her circumstances, but that's only if Mike is willing. I believe he will be. My husband has not shown me that he is willing to change and until he's ready, or God says differently, I will be with him. I know that doesn't sound like the best thing, but this is my season right now.

Some seasons don't look so good. Winter sets in and the cold, harsh realities of life cause us to retreat inside ourselves. I have to continue to stay in the warmth of love. I have to continue to embrace, and to plant, and to build, and to laugh, and to move on by faith. Does that answer your question, LaTicia?"

LaTicia lifted her head, got up from her seat and went around the table to hug First Lady. She needed to hear that. She needed reassurance that First Lady was okay. She had come to question whether or not she herself was capable of having a loving husband if First Lady couldn't make her marriage work. But from everything she had heard First Lady say tonight, she knew she had to focus more on God and on herself, and no matter what happened, good or bad, she could handle any season that came along. She would be unbroken.

PART 3
God Speaks Through The Wind

CHAPTER SIXTEEN

A Summer Breeze

Before Thomas and I married, or even thought about it, I would go walking every morning after my devotion. It was my time to get more in touch with God, to hear His voice, to enjoy His creation, and to gain a more balanced connection for the day ahead. Walking alone was never an issue for me. But on one morning, I passed a lady who was very friendly. She waved and kept going. She seemed to have a level of joy not seen very often.

After a week of passing each other, I decided that if I saw her again the next week, I would introduce myself. I'm so glad I did. It turned out to be a match made in heaven. I knew God had placed her on my path for a reason.

Windella "Weezy" Armstrong was a true woman of God. She shared with me that her nickname was a mix between the first letter of her first name and the word breezy. Her older brother nicknamed her Weezy because she always took things in stride. She never seemed phased by most things and even when she was upset she was still as cool as a breeze.

When I asked how it happened that she was so calm about life she had no problem explaining. "Well, when I was twelve years old, we were in Sunday school, and we sang "Jesus Loves Me," but when we got to the part where it says 'for the Bible tells me so' I wanted to know what that meant so I asked my Sunday school teacher. She opened the Bible and read the story of Jesus's crucifixion. I decided right then and there that if Jesus loved me enough to die for me, then He loves me enough to take care of me no matter what. Right then I decided that whatever happens I would ask Him to help me and I would be alright."

"Wow! The faith of a child."

All I could do was shake my head and silently

think about what she had just told me. I looked down at my promise ring, and it had even more meaning at that moment. I had more of a sense of God's grace because I knew that the time we spent together since making my promise was such a time of peace in my life. It reminded me to not worry about a relationship or anything else. That's when I showed Weezy my promise ring and told her what it meant to me.

"That sounds like a good way to stay in touch with your faith," she said. "I chose not to get married many years ago. Now, at sixty-five, to this day I still believe I made the right decision."

"Oh. You never wanted a husband or children, a family of your own?"

"I thought about maybe missing out on raising children of my own. My older sisters got married and started having children really early, so I was an Aunt pretty young. Taking care of them was nice, and has been a saving grace over the years because children remind you of the innocence and purity we need in our faith, but I also got to see the major responsibility it was to rear children in the image of God. I also saw that you have to have a Godly man in the home and the two must work together or it would be a really hard life. Besides, after my mom passed, I took in my aunt, and I guess you could say she is the child I never had."

"So, you never met the right man? One who you could see yourself raising the kind of family you thought about?"

"When I grew up there were a lot of people getting married young because they got pregnant. This was supposed to be the "right thing," but to me, it was all so backwards. After dating several guys, it became clear to me that they expected sex before marriage no matter how much they went to church, were deacons, pastors, good boys, or whatever. From the time, I was eighteen until I was twenty-one I never met one man who was willing to wait. I did have a few to propose to me, but I knew it was just so we could have sex. I had seen a lot of my friends dumped after they gave in because of a proposal. They were devastated to lose their virginity behind a trick. It was all so evil to me."

"Yes, I can see how that would make you think twice. So what made you finally give up?"

"I wouldn't exactly say I gave up. I just decided being married wasn't as much of priority to me. I wanted to focus more on showing others Christ. When I read Corinthians 7:34, it helped me make up my mind. It says, *'There is a difference also between a wife and a virgin. The unmarried woman cares for the things of the Lord that she may be holy both in body and in spirit: but she who is married cares for the things of the world, how she may please her husband.'* After that, I never regretted my decision."

"That's incredible. So, I'm sure people ask you if you get lonely or do you miss sex, right?"

"Yes, and I tell them that my life is full and rich and I rarely get lonely. But if I do, I can always sing a song, pray, read my word, or call up my family or friends and that goes away."

We laughed and continued our walk for another few minutes. I was absolutely floored at her willingness to follow God at all costs. What a huge sacrifice. It was a testimony I'd never heard before. But, I had been married before, and I loved being a wife. Surely, God would not choose the same path for me as he had chosen for Sister Weezy.

As we made plans to meet at the same time the next day, I walked away feeling like I had been hugged by a summer breeze. I thanked God for sending someone whose faith was so strong. It was a way to stay encouraged in my own promise to wait on God for marriage. From then on Weezy became my sounding board like no one else. Even though she had never been married, her knowledge of scripture made her an authority on life issues in a way that many couldn't articulate. There was nothing I talked to her about that she couldn't guide me to the Word to help me understand God's meaning for it or how to apply the faith I needed to make it through. I knew that God had given me a friend for life, someone of my equal and someone who understood me.

"Thank you, Lord. Thank you for Weezy," I whispered.

CHAPTER SEVENTEEN

And the Wind Blew

It had always been my mission, from day one of my marriage, for Thomas to know I was someone he could trust like no one he'd ever had in his life before. Yet, throughout the course of our marriage, I would find out things that he should have trusted me enough to tell me. It always made me question whether or not I was proving myself enough. Was there anything more I could do to get him to open up?

I found out Thomas did not have a driver's license one night when we were on our way home to Clearville after a service at the church. There was a checkpoint set up, and when the officer asked him for his license, registration, and insurance, he said, "I do not have a license." The officer asked him to step out the car.

When the officer came back, he said, "We will be taking Mr. Brand to the county jail. We have a warrant for his arrest."

Apparently, Thomas had missed court for driving while his license was revoked and did not pay the ticket. It was late on a Friday night, and the probate office would not be open until Monday morning. I used some of my connections and was able to get the clerk at the probate office to agree to meet me at the office Saturday morning and allow me to pay his fees, but he would have to stay in jail Friday night and would not be released unless I paid $675.00 the next day. I borrowed the money from a Sister Weezy because my bank was closed and they would not accept a check. I met with the clerk early that Saturday and paid his fines, and he was at our home in Clearville later that day.

On that day, for the first time in a long time, I saw the man I married. He was so humble; so sweet, so loving. I truly thought this would be a turning point for us. He had seen that I had his back no matter what and that was better than anything that anyone else was offering. We were united, and I saw hope once again.

That only lasted for about a month. After that he was right back to being someone I did not know.

I was awakened to a slam of the door that was so hard it shook the walls and knocked pictures to the floor. I rushed into the office to find Thomas pacing back and forth fuming with anger. When he saw me coming, he looked at me with disgust and turned his back to me.

"Take yourself back in that room."

"Why? What's wrong?"

"Just go back in that room. You know what you did."

"Thomas, I have no idea what you're talking about. What happened?" At this point, I was frantically searching my mind for what I could've done to cause this much anger, but drew a blank.

It was the first night we had spent together in weeks. When he banned me from services, I thought everything was all over. I would call him every day and just act like everything was okay. He still allowed me to talk to him but his tone was cold, and our conversations were always brief. I just wanted him to know that I was still in it, no matter what the devil was trying to do to come between us. I really felt in my heart that Thomas loved me, he had just gotten caught up, and the enemy was using it so we couldn't be that spiritual power couple I always dreamed about. When he called to ask if I wanted to come down and spend some time together, I was overjoyed. I thought God had answered my prayer.

Our night together was spent like old times. Thomas made his infamous tuna salad, and we cuddled and watched movies. We laughed and talked and caught up on some of the things going on at the church. That's when he told me about a few investments he had made for the church that didn't pan out. He had used his rent money, car note, and phone bill money to pay for it. He was worried about how he was going to catch back up. I assured him that I would make sure those things got paid. I wanted him always to remember that I had his back and as long as we were together, he never had to worry.

I stood there, watching Thomas's shoulders heave up and down because he was breathing so hard. His back was still to me. His fists were clenched. I became frightened that I had done something truly horrible and our new beginning would be over just like that.

Thomas turned to me slowly, with his lips barely

open he said, "You told them women down there at that Jezebel meeting about me? That I am mean to you and you are waiting on God to tell you when to leave me?" Flabbergasted and at a loss for words, I blinked and swallowed the lump that had settled in my throat. "Sweetheart, it wasn't like that. I never said it that way. Who told you that?"

"Oh, so you did say it! I knew I couldn't trust you. You just as low down as I said you was. You better be out of here when I come back and if you hold one more of those Jezebel meetings you better not ever let my name come out of your mouth!"

He walked out of the church, slamming the door so hard this time plaster fell from the ceiling, vases fell to the floor, and more pictures fell from the walls. It was just then that I realized the TV was on. Someone on TBN was reading from Matthew 7:26-17, "*And every one who hears these sayings of mine, and does not do them, shall be like a foolish man, who built his house upon the sand: And the rain descended, and the floods came, and the winds blew, and beat on that house; and it fell: and great was its fall.*"

I picked up the remote and turned off the

television. I looked around the room at the things that had fallen, then up at the ceiling where the plaster had come down. I looked beyond that to heaven and asked, "God am I hearing You? I can't be." I slowly went about putting the office back in order and went to the bedroom we had setup at the church to pack my overnight bag and get dressed to leave. Was this the season I had told the ladies at L.I.I.F.T about? Was this God telling me to leave for good? Somehow, I could not let it be that. This was just another test. I would just have to rebuild trust again. I secured the door to the church and walked to my car in a fog.

How quickly the wind blows down a house, but floods happen gradually. Was I being swept away because I was ignoring the rain? I drove home in tears, asking God to speak to me. "Lord, why can't I hear you?"

CHAPTER EIGHTEEN
Carried on a Breeze

That night I lay in bed thinking about Nana and Papa. I found myself twirling my fingers around my wedding band. It dawned on me that I used to do this with the promise ring I had when I was caring for Nana and Papa. Oh, how I missed them. Their passing was crushing to me; first her, then him. I looked down at my wedding band and wondered why my marriage had turned out so opposite of theirs. All those hours learning from them, learning to be alone and happy, getting closer to God. How could this happen?

My heart hurt so bad. I thought long and hard

about what I would do if Thomas called. I wished he would call. I also worried what he would think if I didn't call him. Would he think I didn't care or that I was done? I couldn't stand the thought of him thinking I abandoned him after all he'd been through with his other wives, after telling him I had his back no matter what, and I would always be there for him. I meant every word I said at the altar. Until death do us part was real for me.

I couldn't stand the sadness anymore, so I got down on my knees to pray.

"Heavenly Father, in the name of Jesus I come before you with my heart so broken. Yet Lord, I worship You. I enter into Your presence with thanksgiving because it is only You who has kept me. Lord, You know I desire to do Your will. Not my own. Lord Jesus, You see my heart. You know what I'm going through. Please Lord, until now it seems that I have always heard Your voice. I've always had direction from You, but now I don't know which way to turn. Father, You are not the author of confusion. When I'm confused, I know I must be missing something. Lord, please show me what that is. I can't go on hurting like this, and I don't want to hurt Thomas anymore either. God, I truly believed You put us together. I truly believed You wanted us to minister together and to build a church that would serve so many people around the world. How could I have been so wrong? Lord, You said You would give us the desires of our hearts. My desire is to be with my husband and to make our marriage work; to show him what it's really like to be loved. Please show me what to do to help him see how much I love him. Please, Lord. In the name of Jesus. Amen."

At that moment all I wanted was to soak up the word of God. I went to my desk and opened my Bible. Suddenly, a breeze swept into the window. The wind picked up the copy of our vows that I kept in the Bible to remind me to stand strong in my marriage. I reached to grab the paper, but I couldn't catch it in time. It was carried out of the window on a breeze, swirling through the air. I watched as a cardinal came and flew in circles around it as if they were dancing. Soon, the paper with the words of our promises to always love and cherish one another was out of sight. A single tear escaped my eye, as I looked down at the pages opened in front of me. *'And the wind blew, and the storm came and blew upon that house, and great was the fall of it.'* I closed my Bible and went back to bed, crying myself to sleep. I didn't want to believe what I knew was my answer. I just couldn't let go yet.

CHAPTER NINETEEN

Birds of a Feather

"Mama, guess who I saw Pastor Thomas with this morning at the Jett Pepp?" Sasha said, seemingly disgusted as she talked with her mother of the phone.

"Who?"

"Pastor Sykes! Grady Sykes from Million Mile Church."

"Well Sasha, he and Thomas have been friends since childhood."

"Yes, but I didn't know they ran together like that. Why would he be hanging with him? Everybody knows Grady run women and only God knows what else."

"Those are just rumors. You know I don't like to gossip about people."

"Mom, those are not just rumors. He does this stuff in the open; he doesn't try to hide it. All his baby mamas go to his church."

"Well, I'm sure Thomas had a good reason for being with him."

"He might have had a reason, but I can't say it was a good one."

We laughed, and I changed the subject, all the while keeping what Sasha had said in the back of my mind. It was true. It was highly unlikely that Thomas being with Grady was a good thing. I remembered that was something he did when his other marriages ended. He would hang out with Grady for a few weeks then he would end up at my house for a spiritual retreat to get himself together.

I hadn't noticed the pattern before. I guess it was just something I became accustomed to and didn't really think about. I was too busy focusing on the fact that he was trying to come back to God, not on what he had done to get that point. I immediately felt guilty. It shouldn't matter what he had done before. I didn't want to judge him. I remembered that my sister would always say to, 'Watch the before just as much as you do the after.' I never truly understood what she meant until now.

I got off the phone and sat at my desk to think for a moment. My imagination started getting the best of me as I thought about Thomas and Grady riding around together, making stops at some of the trap houses, bootleggers, and the homes of some of the "fast" women Grady was known to frequent. I could see them sitting around laughing and having a good time while I was at home crying myself to sleep every night. For the first time in my marriage, I started to get resentful. I was relieved when Mr. Miller knocked on my door and brought me back to reality.

"Hey Viveca, did you get those reports back from the U.S.D.A yet?"

"Yes. I emailed them to you when I got here."

"Oh, I haven't checked my email yet. Everything looks good? You think we'll get that contract?"

"Everything looks good. I can't see why we wouldn't."

"Great. I'll go check them out. Thanks!"

"You're welcome. Let me know what you think

when you do."

As I put my head down to start working again, a calm came over me. It was like a sense of freedom I hadn't felt since before I got married. I realized that it was because I had been able to really put my all into my work again over the past few weeks. I was getting my finances back together and feeling a lot better since Weezy and I were walking in the mornings. For the first time in a long time, I felt content.

My mind wandered back to Thomas. I felt sorry for him. I thought about how hard I had tried to help him. How much of myself I had given to help him find himself; to help him see his purpose in God. I thought about him in some hole-in-the-wall with Grady. What a shame. Two pastors, men of God, running the streets. What must it be doing to the sheep they are supposed to shepherd? My heart went out to them.

It occurred to me that it was all in God's hands now. Thomas was caught up with something I absolutely could not help him with. I wanted him to soar like an eagle, and he was running with chickens. Oh well, birds of a feather flock together. I whispered a prayer and went back to work.

CHAPTER TWENTY

Before Dawn

That night, for the first time in ages, I went to bed without feeling tired, stressed, and broken. I don't know why God let Sasha see Thomas at the Jett Pepp that morning. She hardly ever went on that side of town, but she was picking up a co-worker who needed a ride to work. It's funny how He works the simplest things out for our good.

As I lay in bed, I didn't know what to think about this new feeling of peace I had, but it was long overdue. I couldn't believe how much all this had cost me. Besides my savings and self-esteem, for the first time in my daughter's life, she saw my strength fail. That was something I had never wanted her to see. I never wanted my daughter to feel the helplessness I was experiencing. I had to get back to the strength she had always known. I had to do that whether I was with Thomas or not. I had to make up my mind to come from behind the mask once and for all.

The next morning, I was awakened by what felt like a hand gently touching my cheek. I opened my eyes to sunshine and a slight breeze brushing across my face. I wasn't fully awake, so it took me a while to realize I was mixing up the birds chirping with the telephone ringing.

"Hello?"

"Viv, you up?"

"I am now, Thomas. Good morning."

"Good morning. How you doing?"

"I'm okay, and you?"

"I'm good. You still mad at me?"

"I was not mad at you. You were mad at me, remember?"

"Oh yeah. Well, I'm not anymore. I was thinking we should take things slow and just start talking again. You know, maybe talk at night before you go to bed. What you think?"

"I'm open to that."

"Good. The only thing is, they 'bout to cut my phone off. You think you can pay the bill for me so we can really work on things?"

"How much is it?"

"It's just sixty dollars."

"Okay, let me get up and get myself together, and I'll call them to pay it and call you back to let you know when it's done."

"Praise God. Thank you, Baby."

"You're welcome, Thomas."

I hung up the phone and lay there for a few seconds. I decided not to think too long about what just happened and went to the bathroom to wash my face and brush my teeth. I went into the kitchen, made a cup of coffee, got my debit card out of my purse, and sat down at the table to make the payment. Afterwards, I sat sipping my coffee and listening to the birds chirping.

Staring out the window at the fallen magnolia leaves, I thanked God for not letting me become bitter after all I had gone through with Thomas. I decided that whether this was really a turning point or not, this would be my prayer; "Lord, please don't let me be bitter no matter what happens from this point on. Just keep my heart open to love. Amen."

I called Thomas back to let him know I had paid the bill.

"Thank you, Baby. You have always had my back. I'm going to do the same for you.

"You're welcome. I'm going to go ahead and get ready for work."

"Okay, I'll call you tonight about eight o'clock. Have a good day at work."

"Thank you. I will."

I went to work content, but only slightly hopeful. I knew it seemed that I was being naive by paying his bill. It was hard to say how this would turn out because there were times when he would ask me for things and then when I gave them to him he would act disgusted with me. I came to understand that it was because he was so accustomed to drama and coming by everything the hard way, that it wasn't easy for him to accept having someone who was trying to show God's easy love by giving as our Father gives. I think Thomas had a hard time believing someone could love him and give to him without any demands or motives.

CHAPTER TWENTY-ONE

Far Be It

I had a wonderful day at work and stopped by the grocery store. The plan was to come home, cook myself a nice meal, and relax while I waited for Thomas to call. I got home about six-thirty. With an hour and a half left, I put away the groceries, took a shower, and went into the kitchen to cook. Just as I was preparing to put my food on the plate, the phone rang.

"Oh Sweetheart, you're early. I was just about to have dinner. Wish you were here." I said with a smile, hoping he could sense it.

"Yeah, I'm early because I don't want to waste any more time. I'm just gon' be point blank. To stay with you, I need more."

"More what?"

"What you got?"

"What do you mean, what do I got?"

"What do you got for me to stay with you? I know you still got that weight. You still big as ever even though you said you was gon' lose it. You got time to come back and forth to see me? Because I ain't using my gas to come that way. I still can't get you to freak me like I want. So, what you got?"

The usual fear, hurt, and disappointment I felt when he talked to me this way was replaced by frustration and anger. I took a few deep breaths and prayed in my mind. The last thing I wanted was to give him another excuse to say it was my fault things ended the way they usually did. I took one last deep breath.

"Thomas. I thank God that He has given me the strength to endure all that we have been through. There has been such deep hurt that only tears and God could heal. I wish I could say that I had a lot more to offer you, but even the tears have dried up. So, if you want me just as I am, just me, just as God made me, then that's all I got. By His standards, I think that's enough!"

It was the first time in our marriage I didn't crumble at his hurtful words. It was also the first time he did not immediately come back with more hurtful words. The silence on the other end of the phone was deafening.

"I see. So, you saying you good?"

"I don't know what you mean. You asked what I have, and I told you. You just have to decide if it's enough."

"Well, I guess I'm done then. You played yourself. I'm through with you. I don't even know why I married you in the first place. Don't call me for nothing. I don't wanna hear from you again and you better not talk to my daughter no more either. I don't want you filling her head with your garbage. You're so stupid to be so smart. It is hard to be a husband and a pastor. If I had known God was going to give me a church of my own so quickly, I would never have married you."

I just held the phone. I had no reply. What more was there to say? I listened to hear if there was anything from the voice of God. I heard nothing, so I said nothing.

"Bye!" Thomas yelled as he hung up.

I sat down at the table watching the phone in my now shaking hand. All of the penned up feelings that hadn't come out through my tears now came out in a fit of shaking and shortness of breath.

It took a while, but I got myself together. In a bit of a daze, I fixed my plate and sat down to eat, but realized I had lost my appetite. The glare from my wedding band kept catching my eye, so I removed it from my hand and attempted to continue on with my meal. With each bite I took, I remembered where I had been before Thomas asked me to marry him. I was in agreement with God that my heart mattered and that it belonged to Him.

At that moment, I realized that even with God I had been wearing a mask. Even though I was transparent with Him about my pain, I was not honest with Him about what was causing my pain. A scripture, John 3, came to mind: *"The wind blows where it will, and you hear the sound of it, but can not tell where it came from, or where it is going: so is everyone who is born of the Spirit."*

I asked God to forgive me. All along, He had been speaking to me, but I was so busy trying to hold on to a lie and did not realize I had stopped telling myself and Him the truth. For that reason, I was no longer able to be who He made me to be. It was time for a spiritual rebirth.

"God, please forgive me. I only wanted to serve You and do Your will. I understand now that I couldn't do that with a man who didn't know how to love himself. Therefore he couldn't really love me. Because of that, my love for me faded, and I could no longer be honest with You. I'm sorry, Lord. Help me to see my way back to me. Help me to remove the masks once and for all. Far be it from me to ever lie to You or myself again. By Your grace, I will worship You in spirit and in truth from here on. In Jesus name. Amen."

CHAPTER TWENTY-TWO

Ushered

Months later, I sat at my granddaughter's kindergarten graduation watching her beam. I looked over at my daughter and her husband who were glowing while watching their child. I felt the love and respect from them that I had before my marriage. Not that their love and respect went away, but now I felt worthy of it again.

I hadn't heard much from Thomas since our last conversation. I put my wedding rings in a safe deposit box away from the house. I didn't want to see them and be tempted to reminisce and wish for something that was not possible.

I stopped wondering why I had made such a huge mistake and started thanking God that I had come out of it with my faith still intact. I was grateful to still have my job and I was happy that I was able to go back to Mt. Sharon and be welcomed with opened arms.

The first time I was ushered in to preach, I was right at home. I did have quite a testimony, but I was not yet ready to share it because I was still going through the healing process. Nevertheless, I allowed the word of God to bring me back into one hundred percent truth with Him and to pass that truth through me to the church. Many people got delivered.

After the graduation, we gathered around to take pictures. My beautiful, tall, statuesque daughter had all eyes on her. It seemed that even she started to flourish again. I had just recently come to understand how much the pain of my marriage had taken its toll on her as well. To see her shining again, being a strong example for her own daughter, would help me to stay strong when the reality of my pending divorce would hit home.

Even though Mr. Miller and I were business partners, I finally found the courage to venture out and do something I had always wanted to do. I started my own company managing properties. The two businesses definitely kept me too busy to worry about things with Thomas, but they also helped me see the tremendous faith it takes to step out on your own. If my divorce taught me anything, it was that I could handle anything, absolutely anything, if I am willing to be truthful with myself.

Although I feel like I get over Thomas more every day, I'm not so sure I'm getting over being divorced. The thought of it sometimes makes me feel like I'm going against what God designed, but I reminded myself that God only designs the marriages that He puts together. Just because we're Christians doesn't mean we always choose who God wants us to be with; even if they are pastors.

From the outside looking in, being a First Lady can seem glamorous. It can cause some people to think there's a certain level of stature and many pastor's wives are put on pedestals. Sometimes, people don't really get that we're human with real flaws, needs, and worries. They forget that our husbands are regular men; the calling on their lives doesn't define them, it only gives them more of an opportunity to be saved by pulling others out of the enemy's grips.

While I smiled for the camera, with my daughter and granddaughter next to me, it felt good to do so without the mask of a First Lady. I could just be Viv again. With every second of finding myself again, I felt ushered into the presence of God; never again to be abandoned.

Epilogue

Although it seems like First Lady gets over Pastor Thomas a little more each day, I am not sure she is getting over being divorced, or how so many were let down by the issues Pastor Thomas and she had in their marriage. Even though most of us that were scattered have connected to other ministries, she still prays for us more than she does herself. She prays that we will not let the failures we saw in Pastor Thomas, and the fall of our church, make us untrusting or bitter towards other ministries.

I have to remind myself that God can ordain a marriage and a ministry, but even then, he does not force His will on us. He still gives us the ability to choose. This knowledge really helps me on those days when I wonder if I could have done more, as her armor bearer, to help First Lady save her marriage. It takes two to make a marriage work, and both people have to be willing participants. The day Pastor Thomas told First Lady he no longer wanted to be married to her was the day he was no longer a participant. First Lady was left to fight a losing battle.

From the outside looking in, the life of a First Lady might appear glamorous, but the fact of the matter is that First Ladies are wives of men. Pastors have imperfections too and even in marriage; they experience struggles just as any other married couple would, sometimes more. Because of who they are, First Ladies often have to overlook their own desires and expectations for the sake of others. As spiritual mothers, they hold things together even when everything around them is falling apart. They uplift others even when they are being torn down. They encourage others even when they are in a place of discouragement. They pray for others even though they are in much need of prayer. They forgive others even though they are often not forgiven. They are constantly uplifting their husbands, who are also their pastors, in spite of their imperfections; they are constantly praying for a better day.

Most of the time, we as sheep embrace the Pastor but often take the First Lady for granted. We value only her attachment to the Pastor without realizing that First Ladies, by God's grace and mercy, are the glue that holds it all together. Yes, First Ladies are "mothers" to all. At least our First Lady was.

I see Pastor Thomas from time to time, and he says he is happier than he has ever been. He is doing what he seems to love, and although some might turn their heads at his career choice, it is an honest living, and he has always had a wonderful voice. He says he wishes someone would approach him about his singing in a blues band. If it is wrong for him to sing it at events, then it is wrong for them to listen to it in their homes. I guess he has a point there.

First Lady continues to encourage women to support and respect each other. She still visits the sick and shut-in, and on occasion, one of us will receive a card in the mail with a financial blessing inside. There is no return address, but we have all figured out it is First Lady. L.I.I.F.T. continues to be an escape and a place of strength and encouragement for so many.

I saw First Lady a couple months ago at her

granddaughter's kindergarten graduation taking pictures with her daughter and her family. I know it felt good for her to smile without the "mask" of a First Lady. She is Viv again.

I once asked her how she survived it all and she replied, "With every second of finding myself again, I felt ushered into the presence of God even more. Never again to be abandoned."

It is true that what does not break us makes us stronger and sometimes it is in your brokenness that you find out exactly who you are and whose you are. I guess you could say, in her brokenness, she discovered a better version of herself.

A Tribute to the Faithful Ladies of L.I.F.T.
(Ladies Increasing In Faith Together)
Favorite Scriptures – KJV (unless otherwise noted)

Sister M. Baxter (Praise Leader) - Philippians 4:13

Sister T. Dent (Praiser) - Psalm 100

Sister H. Hightower (Blessed Woman of God) - Psalm 39: 1-9-with focus on verse 4

Sister A. Owens (Victorious Woman of God) - Matthew 11:28-30

Sister Y. Cassidy (Servant of the Lord) – Ephesians 6:11 (NIV)

Sister J. Walker (Psalmist for the Lord) – Psalm 100:4

Sister S. Williams (Prayer Warrior) - Matthew 6:33

Sister D. Moore (Awesome Woman of God)- Psalm 37

Sister S. Spencer (Woman of Wisdom) – Psalm 27

Sister M. Holt (Motivator) - Romans 8:28

Sister R. Rodgers (Humble Servant) - Romans 3:23

Sister/Minister D. Mallord (Soul Winner for the Lord)-
Psalm 24

Sister/First Lady W. Jackson (Encourager) - Psalm 23

Founder V. Tracy (Great Ambassador)
Favorite Scripture- KJV Revelation 7:14- *And I said*
unto him, Sir, thou knowest. And he said to me, These
are they which came out of great tribulation, and have
washed their robes, and made them white in the blood
of the Lamb.

About the Author

Vanessa Rodgers Tracy is a minister and a former First Lady. Raised in Brundidge, Alabama, she discovered at an early age that she was powerful with the pen. Her first work was published in 1996 in the National Library of Poetry - A Delicate Balance "Whisper In The Wind". Though she loves writing, she especially loves spending time with her grandbabies Mariah, Martell-II, and Maliah. She hopes this novel will bring encouragement, laughter, and the ability to forgive to its readers.

If you want to learn more about Vanessa's next book, and how you can get a copy, please visit her website at www.vanessartracy.com where you can sign up to receive emails about her next release.

To: Mr. Art
Thank you so much!
for Supporting - Enjoy!
God Bless,

Love,
Vanessa Rodgers Gracy
3/2/2019

Made in the USA
Columbia, SC
31 January 2019